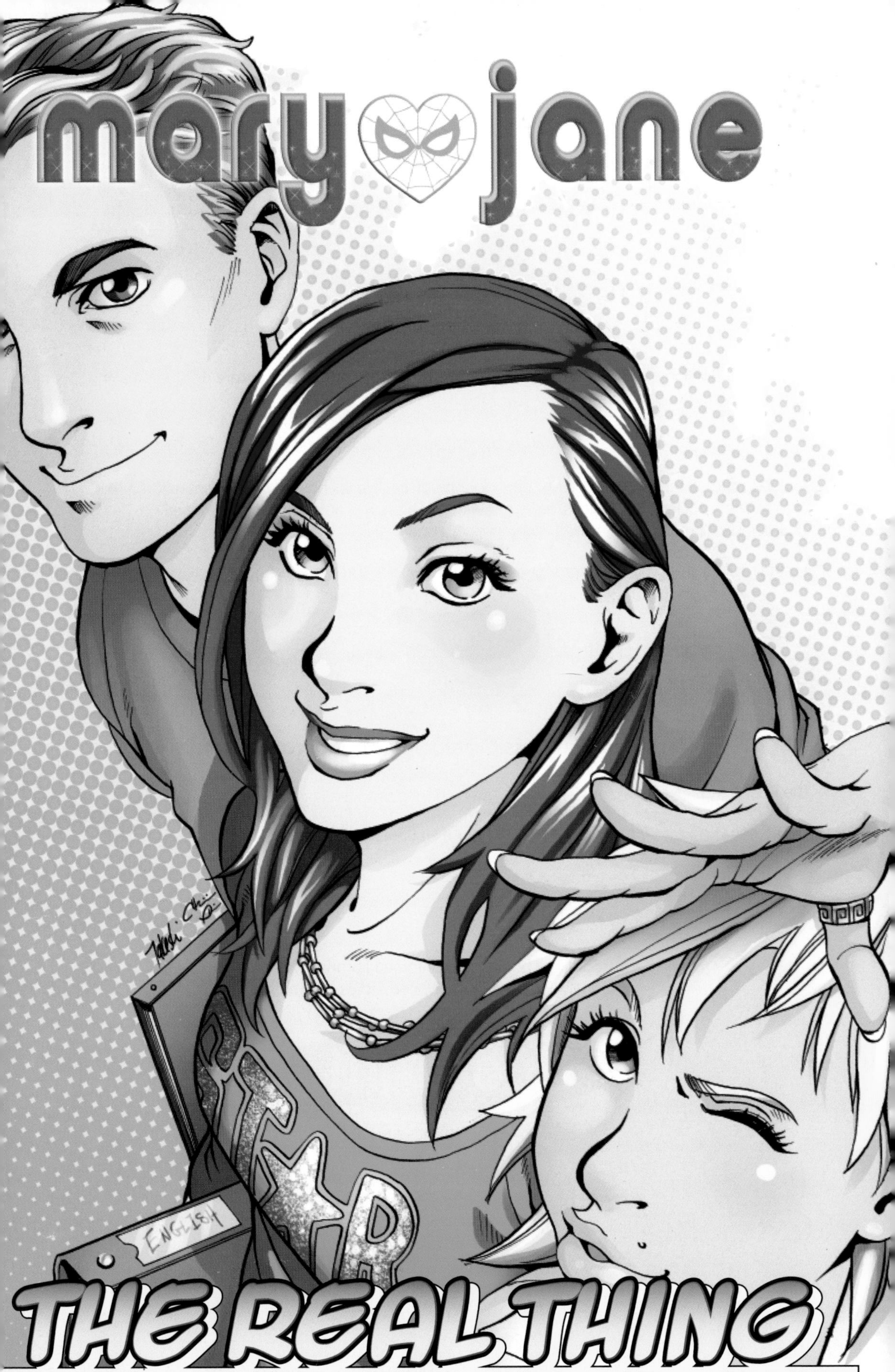
mary jane
ENGLISH

THE REAL THING

Sean cKeever	Takeshi Miyazawa	Norman Lee	Christina Strain	Virtual Calligraphy's Randy Gentile	MacKenzie Cadenhead	C.B. Cebulski	Joe Quesada	Dan Buckley
Writer	Pencils	inks	Colors	Letters	Editor	Consulting Editor	Chief	Publisher

VISIT US AT
www.abdopub.com

Spotlight, a division of ABDO Publishing Company Inc., is the school and library distributor of the Marvel Entertainment books.

Library bound edition © 2006

Library of Congress Cataloging-in-Publication Data

The Real Thing

ISBN 1-59961-039-6 (Reinforced Library Bound Edition)

All Spotlight books are reinforced library binding and manufactured in the United States of America

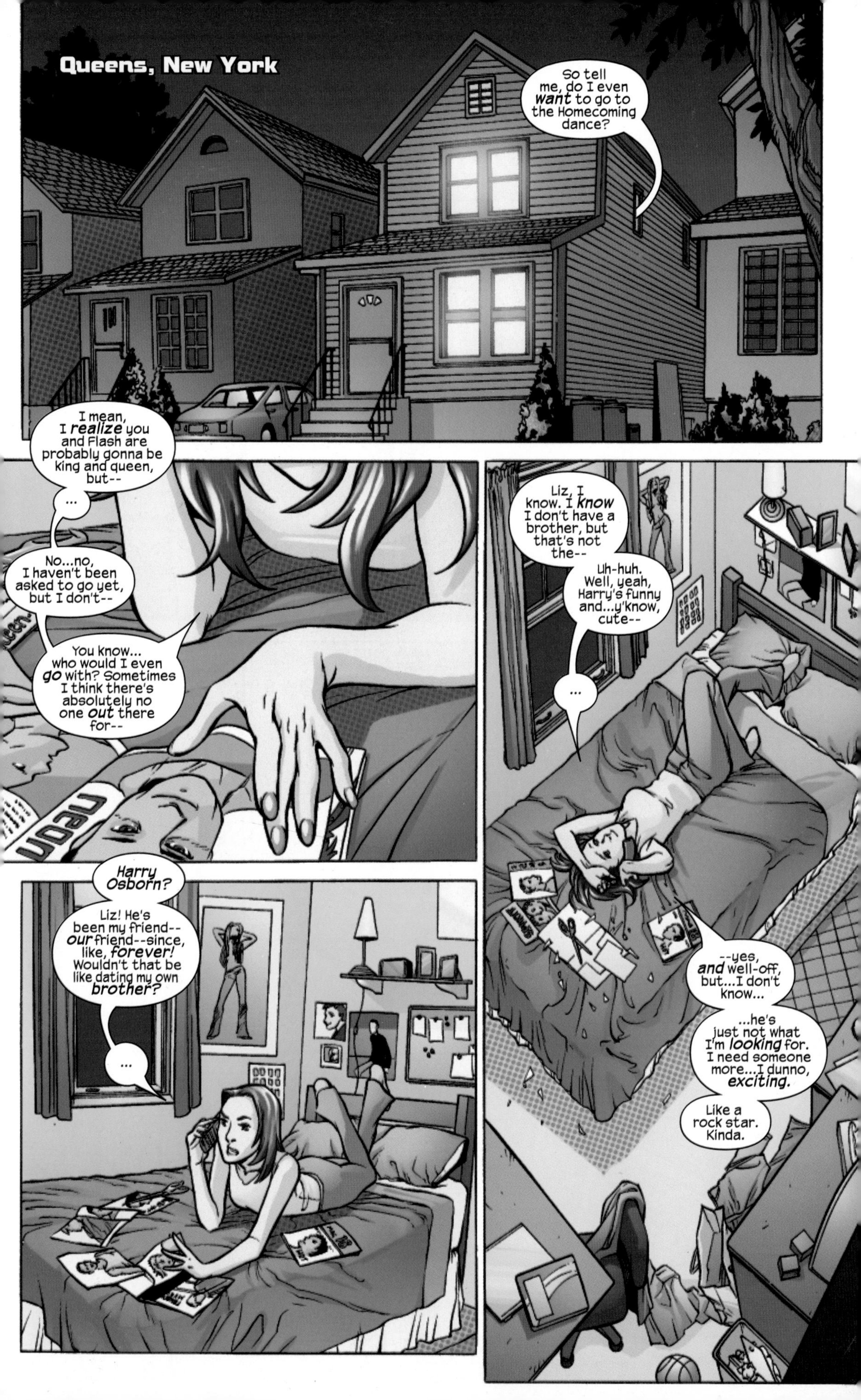
Queens, New York
So tell me, do I even *want* to go to the Homecoming dance?
I mean, I *realize* you and Flash are probably gonna be king and queen, but--
...
No...no, I haven't been asked to go yet, but I don't--
You know... who would I even *go* with? Sometimes I think there's absolutely no one *out* there for--
Harry Osborn?
Liz! He's been my friend-- *our* friend--since, like, *forever!* Wouldn't that be like dating my own *brother?*
...
Liz, I know. I *know* I don't have a brother, but that's not the--
Uh-huh. Well, yeah, Harry's funny and...y'know, cute--
...
--yes, *and* well-off, but...I don't know...
...he's just not what I'm *looking* for. I need someone more...I dunno, *exciting.*
Like a rock star. Kinda.

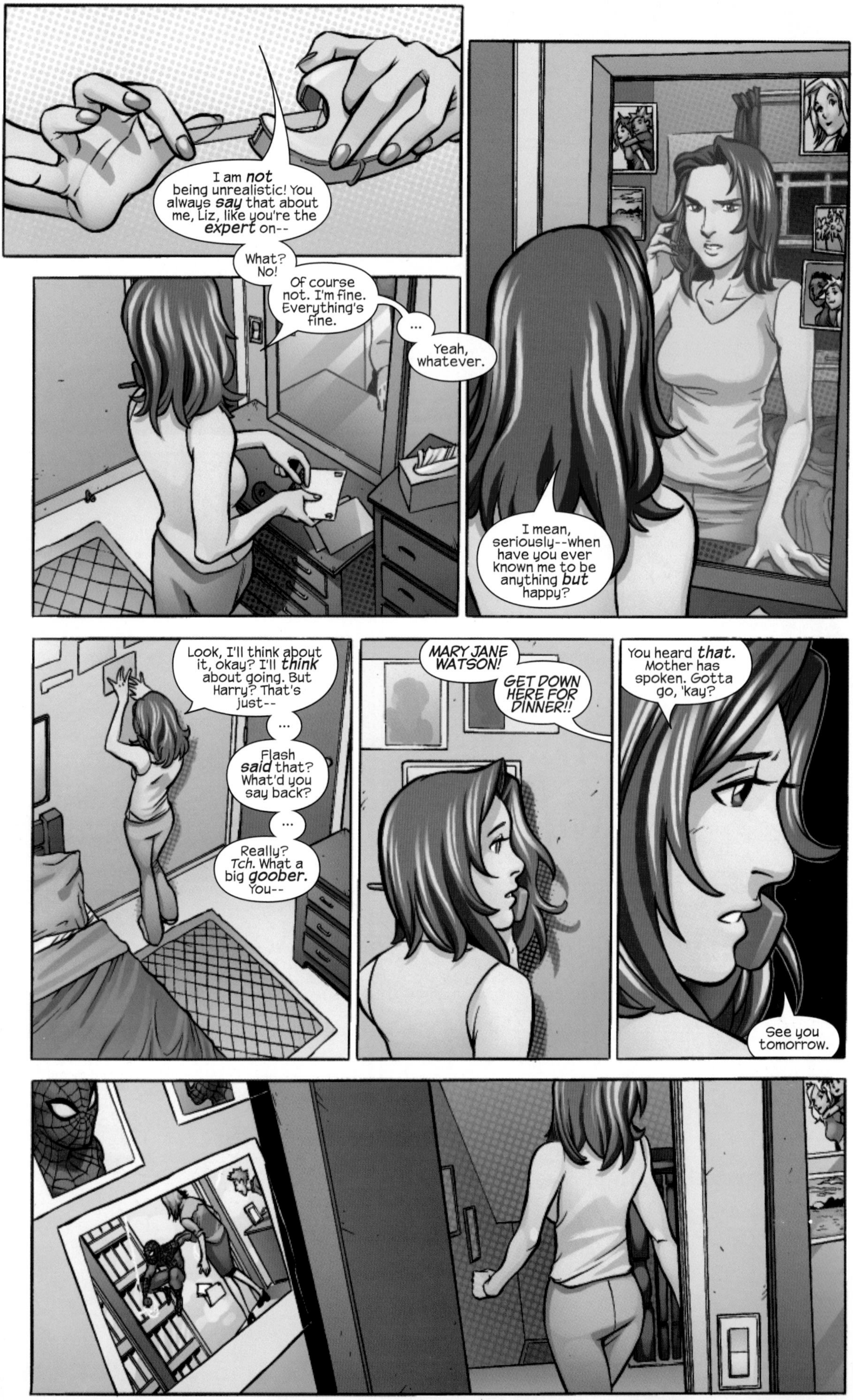

I am **not** being unrealistic! You always **say** that about me, Liz, like you're the **expert** on--
What? No!
Of course not. I'm fine. Everything's fine.
...
Yeah, whatever.
I mean, seriously--when have you ever known me to be anything **but** happy?
Look, I'll think about it, okay? I'll **think** about going. But Harry? That's just--
...
Flash **said** that? What'd you say back?
...
Really? *Tch.* What a big **goober**. You--
MARY JANE WATSON!
GET DOWN HERE FOR DINNER!!
You heard **that.** Mother has spoken. Gotta go, 'kay?
See you tomorrow.

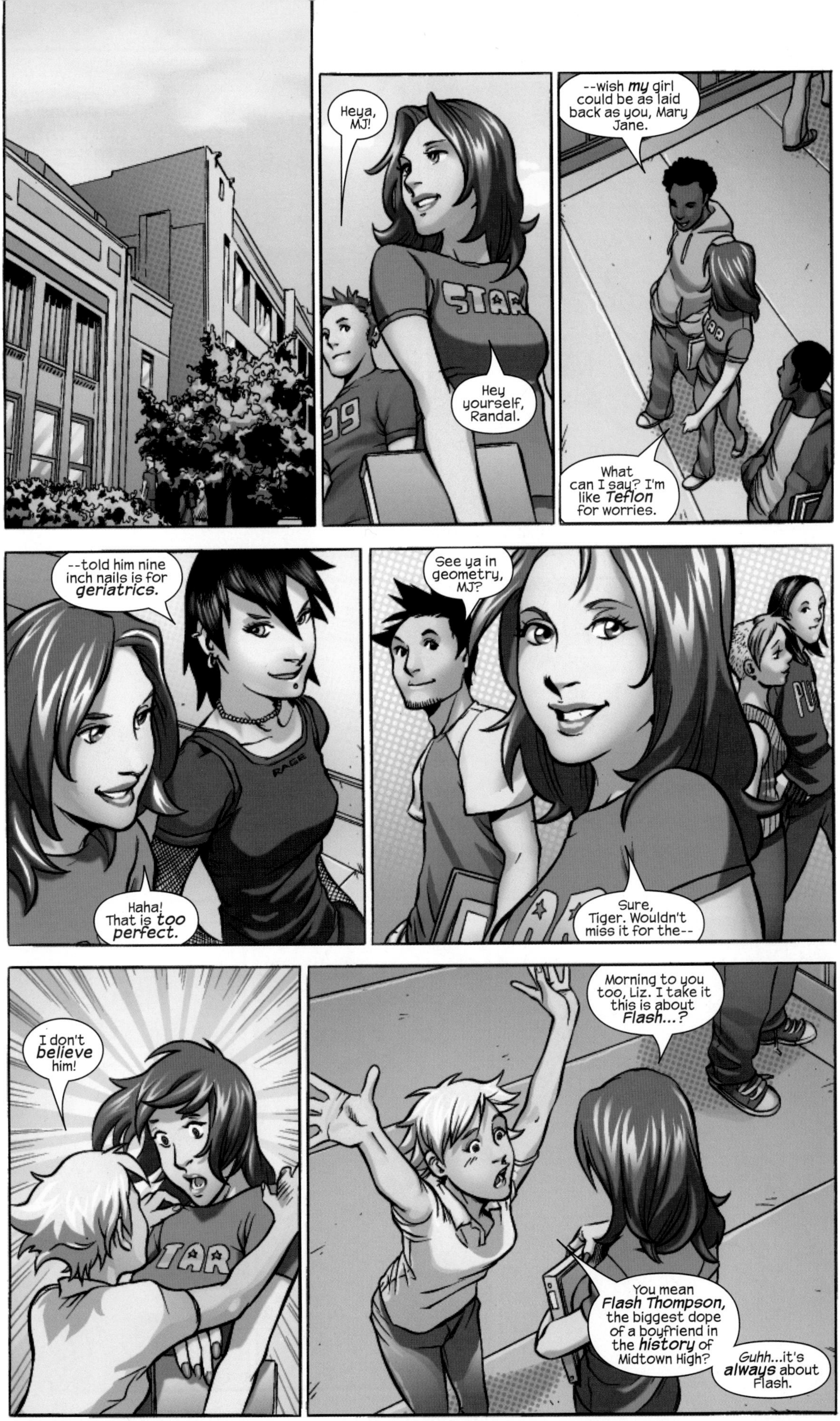
Heya, MJ!
Hey yourself, Randal.
--wish my girl could be as laid back as you, Mary Jane.
What can I say? I'm like Teflon for worries.
--told him nine inch nails is for geriatrics.
Haha! That is too perfect.
See ya in geometry, MJ?
Sure, Tiger. Wouldn't miss it for the--
I don't believe him!
Morning to you too, Liz. I take it this is about Flash...?
You mean Flash Thompson, the biggest dope of a boyfriend in the history of Midtown High?
Guhh...it's always about Flash.

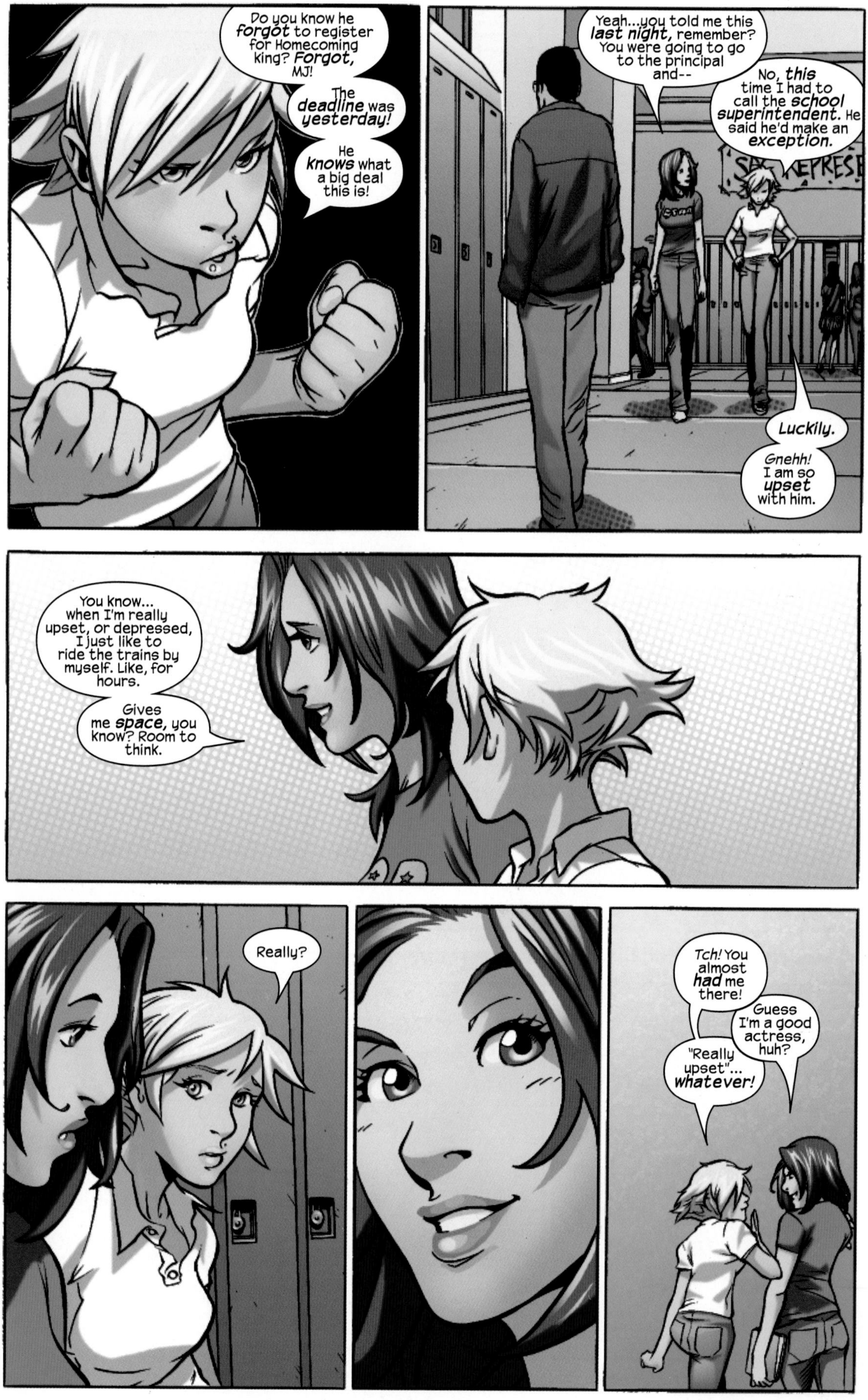
Do you know he forgot to register for Homecoming King? Forgot, MJ!
The deadline was yesterday!
He knows what a big deal this is!
Yeah...you told me this last night, remember? You were going to go to the principal and--
No, this time I had to call the school superintendent. He said he'd make an exception.
Luckily.
Gnehh! I am so upset with him.
You know... when I'm really upset, or depressed, I just like to ride the trains by myself. Like, for hours.
Gives me space, you know? Room to think.
Really?
Tch! You almost had me there!
"Really upset"... whatever!
Guess I'm a good actress, huh?

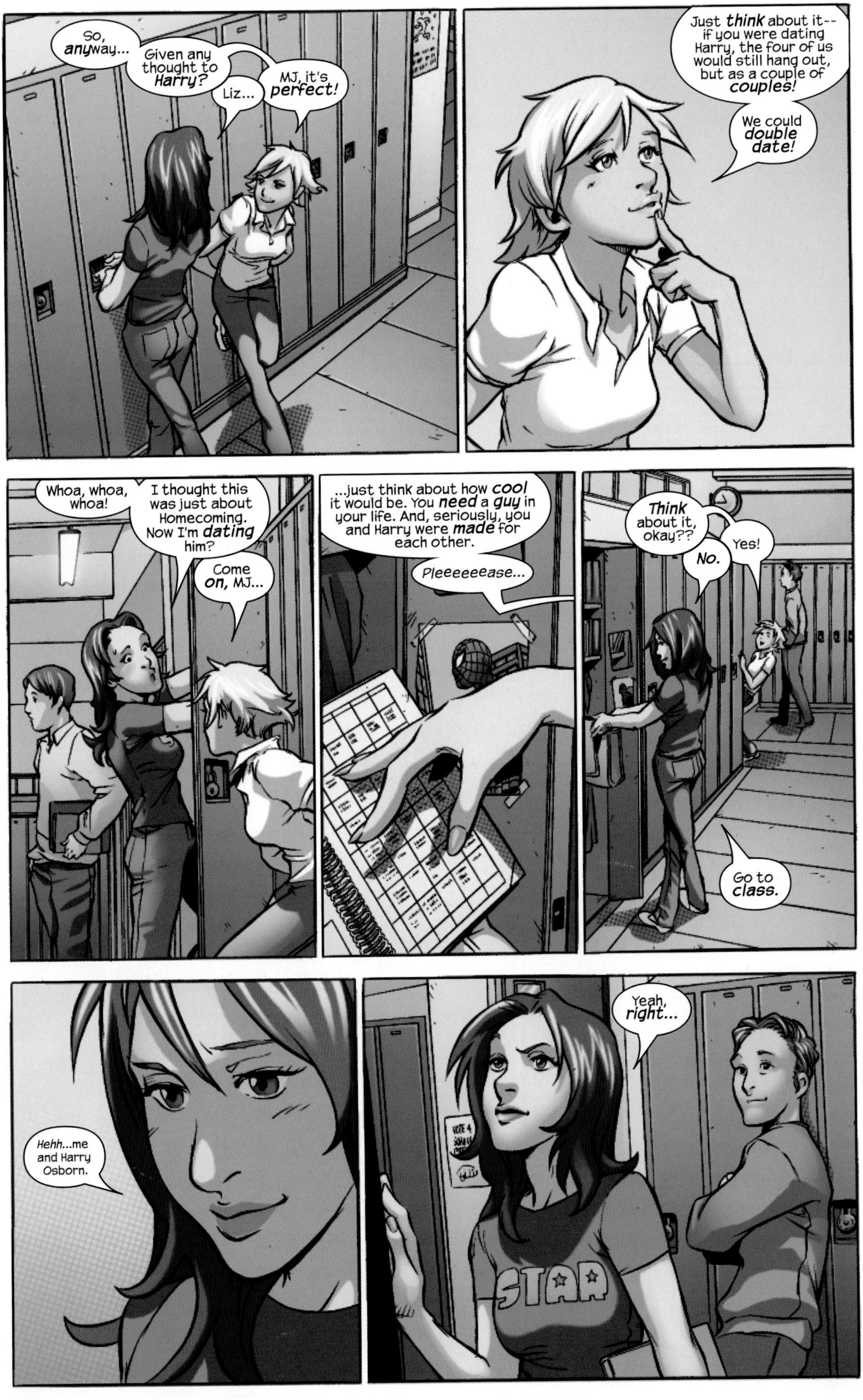
So, anyway...
Given any thought to Harry?
Liz...
MJ, it's perfect!
Just think about it--if you were dating Harry, the four of us would still hang out, but as a couple of couples!
We could double date!
Whoa, whoa, whoa!
I thought this was just about Homecoming. Now I'm dating him?
Come on, MJ...
...just think about how cool it would be. You need a guy in your life. And, seriously, you and Harry were made for each other.
Pleeeeeease...
Think about it, okay??
No.
Yes!
Go to class.
Hehh...me and Harry Osborn.
Yeah, right...
STAR

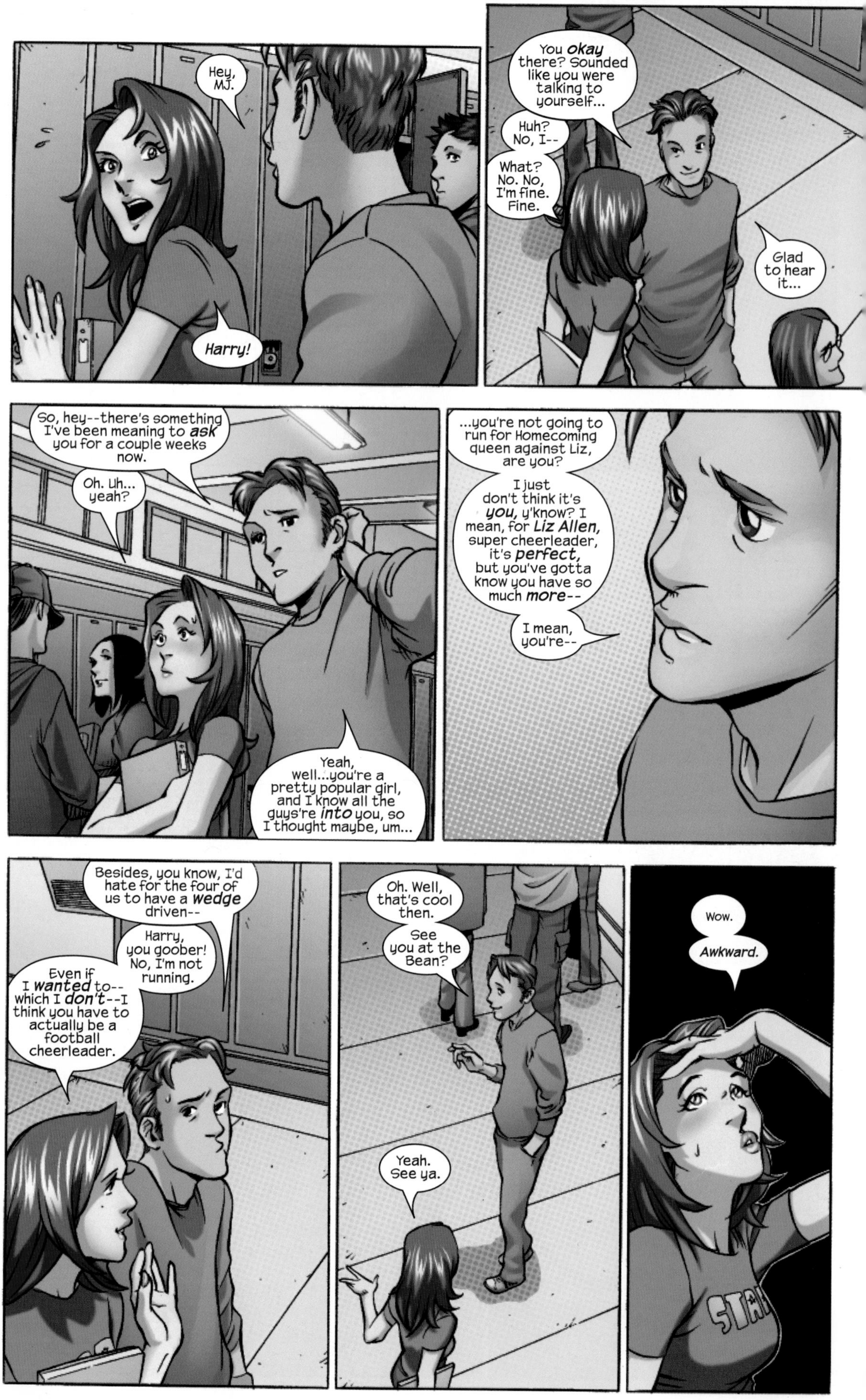
Hey, MJ.
Harry!
You okay there? Sounded like you were talking to yourself...
Huh? No, I--
What? No. No, I'm fine. Fine.
Glad to hear it...
So, hey--there's something I've been meaning to ask you for a couple weeks now.
Oh. Uh... yeah?
Yeah, well...you're a pretty popular girl, and I know all the guys're into you, so I thought maybe, um...
...you're not going to run for Homecoming queen against Liz, are you?
I just don't think it's you, y'know? I mean, for Liz Allen, super cheerleader, it's perfect, but you've gotta know you have so much more--
I mean, you're--
Besides, you know, I'd hate for the four of us to have a wedge driven--
Harry, you goober! No, I'm not running.
Even if I wanted to--which I don't--I think you have to actually be a football cheerleader.
Oh. Well, that's cool then.
See you at the Bean?
Yeah. See ya.
Wow.
Awkward.

Riddle me this...when am I *ever* going to use advanced algebra in real life?

I mean, polynomials, domains...I *tried* to get Mr. Layters to *explain* it to me, but...

I wish I could just *skip* that class altogether.

I hear *that!* Heck, I say we skip 'em *all!*

What I *really* wish I could ditch, though, is this whole Homecoming king garbage.

Flash Thompson.

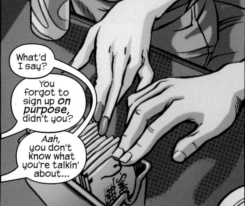

What'd I say?

You forgot to sign up *on purpose*, didn't you?

Aah, you don't know what you're talkin' about...

I don't know what *I'm* talking about? *You're* the big *lunkhead* who doesn't understand words with more than two syllables!

Whatever.

Yeah, whatev--

Hey, Harry.

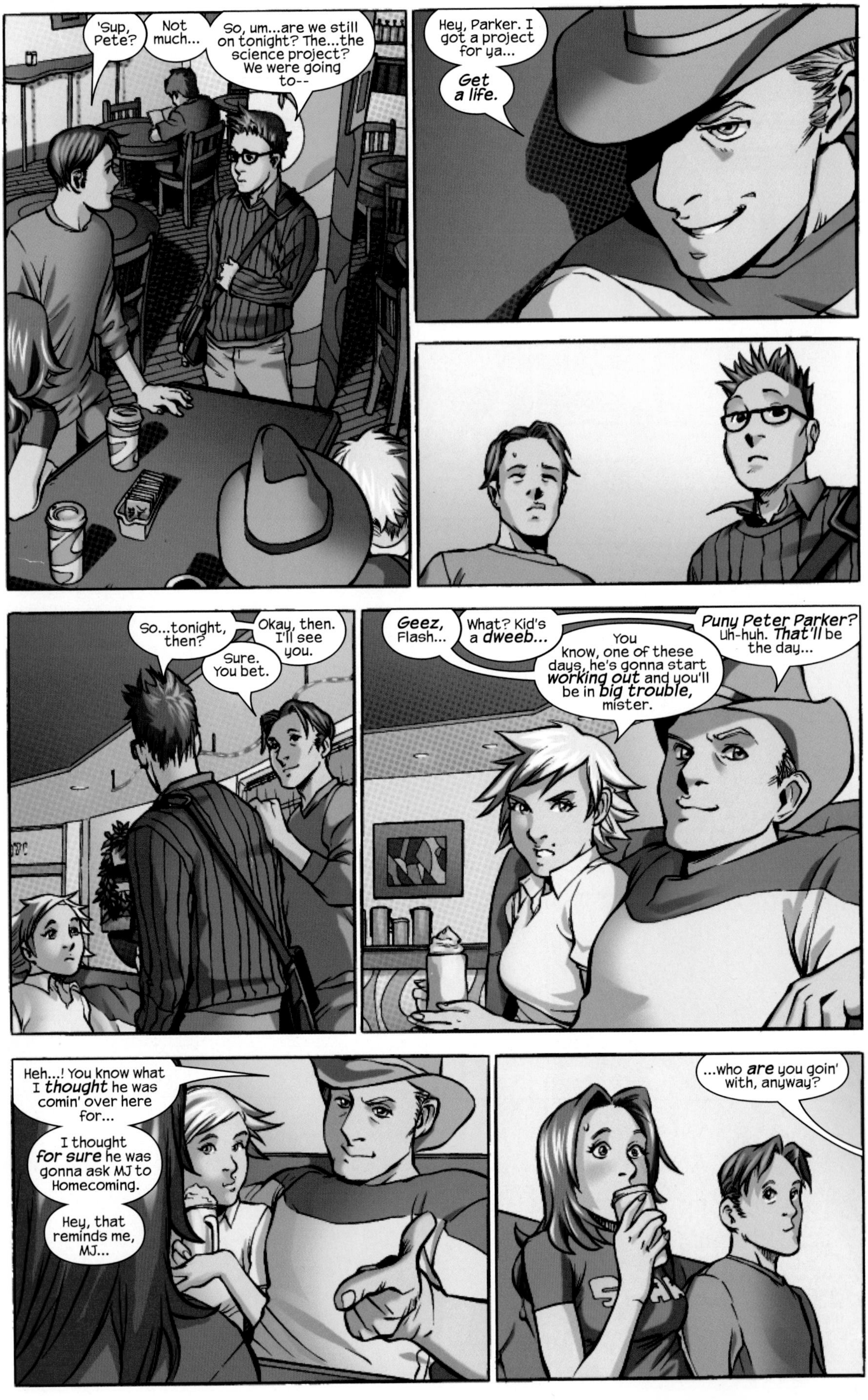
'Sup, Pete?
Not much...
So, um...are we still on tonight? The...the science project? We were going to--
Hey, Parker. I got a project for ya...
Get a life.
So...tonight, then?
Okay, then. I'll see you.
Sure. You bet.
Geez, Flash...
What? Kid's a dweeb...
You know, one of these days, he's gonna start working out and you'll be in big trouble, mister.
Puny Peter Parker? Uh-huh. That'll be the day...
Heh...! You know what I thought he was comin' over here for...
I thought for sure he was gonna ask MJ to Homecoming.
Hey, that reminds me, MJ...
...who are you goin' with, anyway?

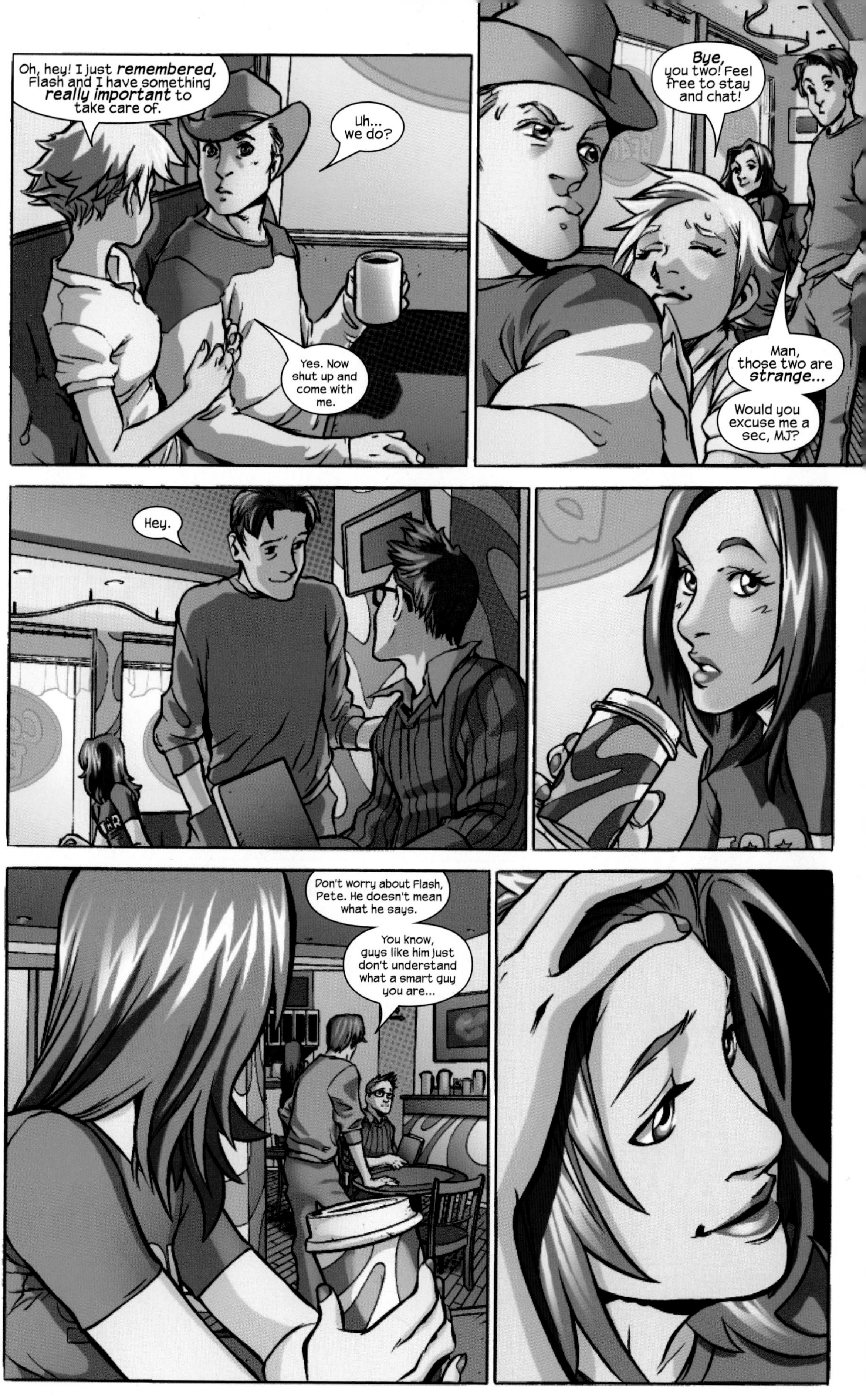
Oh, hey! I just remembered, Flash and I have something really important to take care of.
Uh... we do?
Yes. Now shut up and come with me.
Bye, you two! Feel free to stay and chat!
Man, those two are strange...
Would you excuse me a sec, MJ?
Hey.
Don't worry about Flash, Pete. He doesn't mean what he says.
You know, guys like him just don't understand what a smart guy you are...

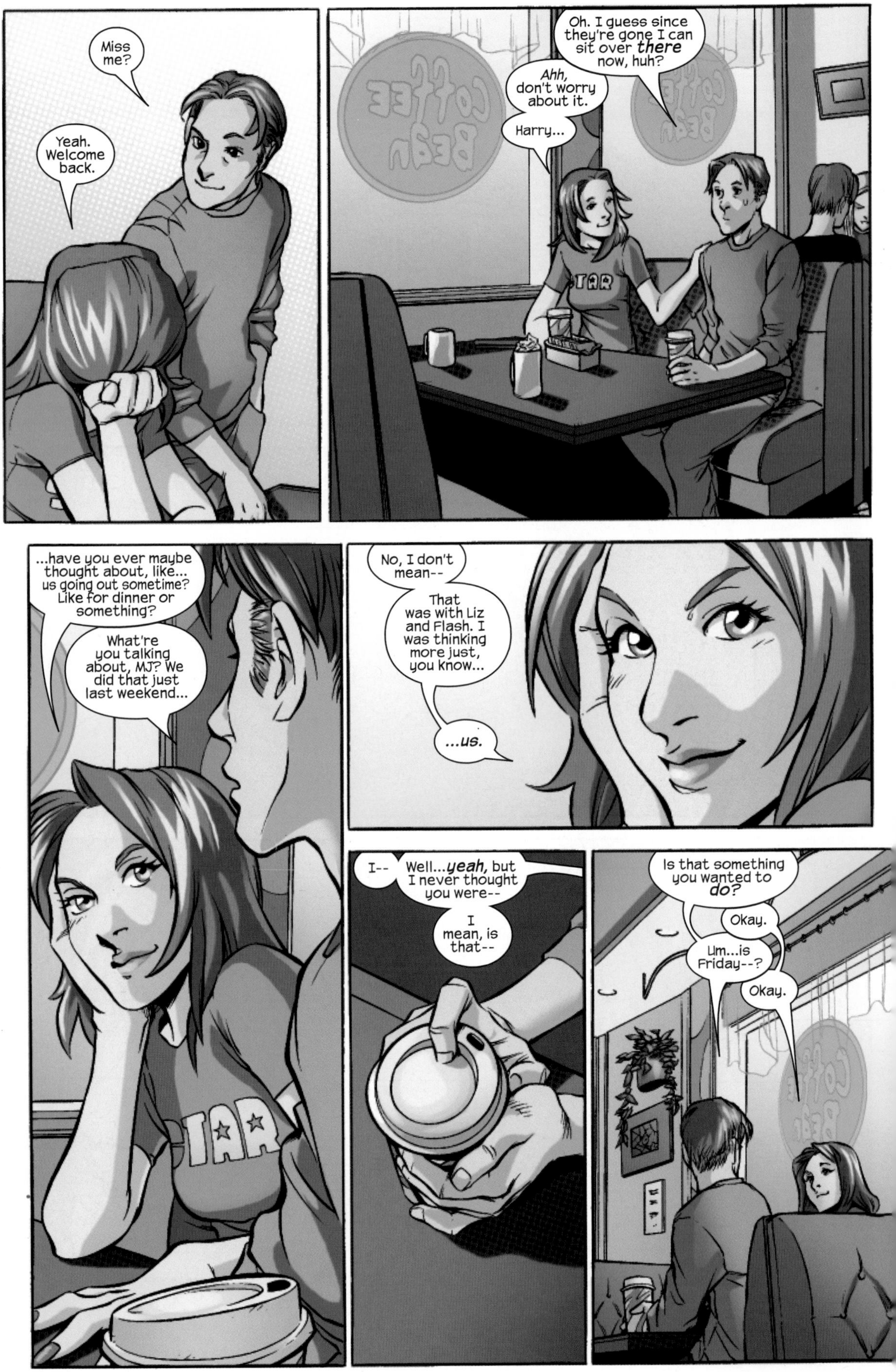
Miss me?
Yeah. Welcome back.
Oh. I guess since they're gone I can sit over *there* now, huh?
Ahh, don't worry about it.
Harry...
...have you ever maybe thought about, like... us going out sometime? Like for dinner or something?
What're you talking about, MJ? We did that just last weekend...
No, I don't mean--
That was with Liz and Flash. I was thinking more just, you know...
...us.
I--
Well...*yeah,* but I never thought you were--
I mean, is that--
Is that something you wanted to *do?*
Okay.
Um...is Friday--?
Okay.

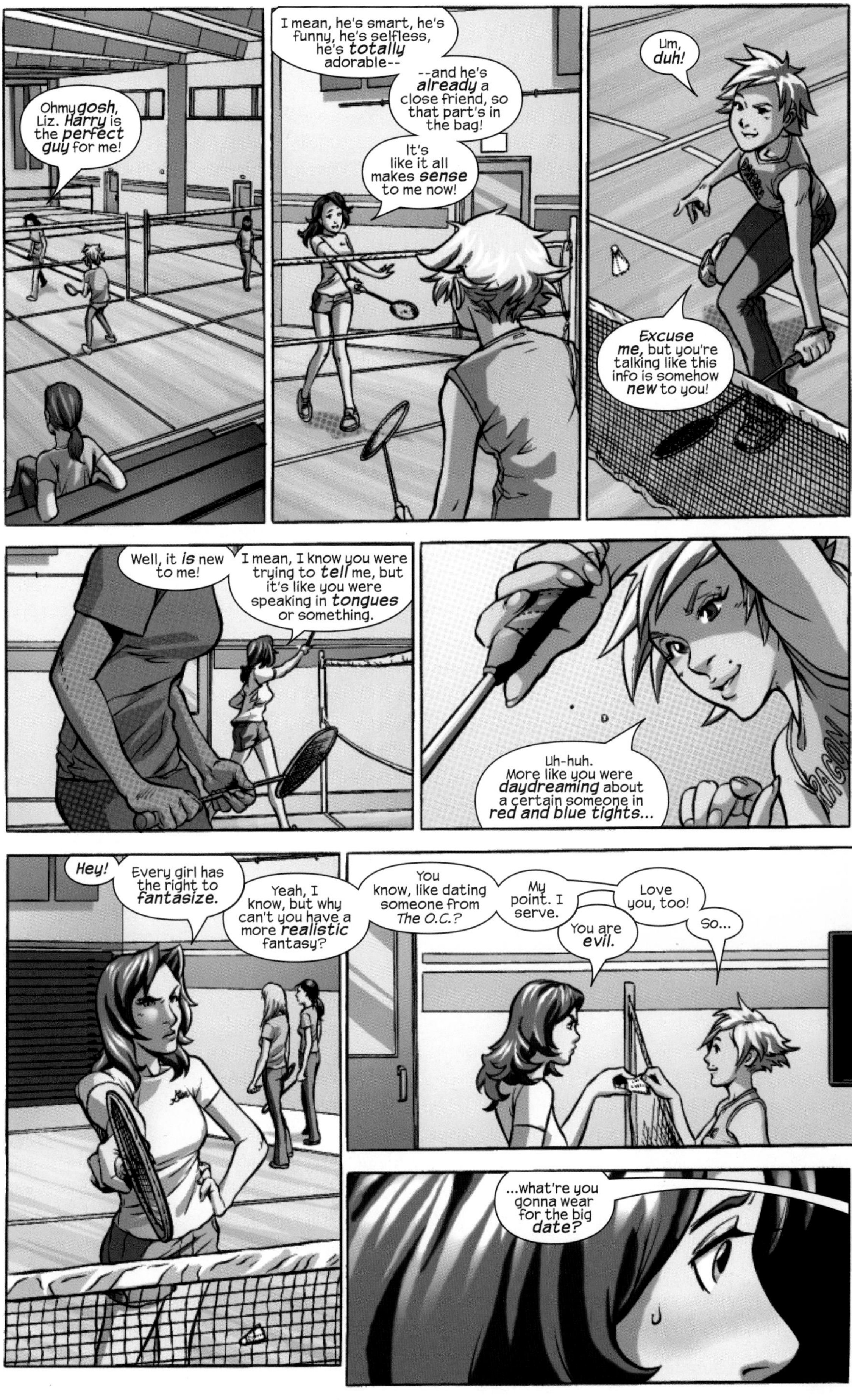
Ohmygosh, Liz. Harry is the perfect guy for me!
I mean, he's smart, he's funny, he's selfless, he's totally adorable--
--and he's already a close friend, so that part's in the bag!
It's like it all makes sense to me now!
Um, duh!
Excuse me, but you're talking like this info is somehow new to you!
Well, it is new to me!
I mean, I know you were trying to tell me, but it's like you were speaking in tongues or something.
Uh-huh. More like you were daydreaming about a certain someone in red and blue tights...
Hey!
Every girl has the right to fantasize.
Yeah, I know, but why can't you have a more realistic fantasy?
You know, like dating someone from The O.C.?
My point. I serve.
Love you, too!
You are evil.
So...
...what're you gonna wear for the big date?

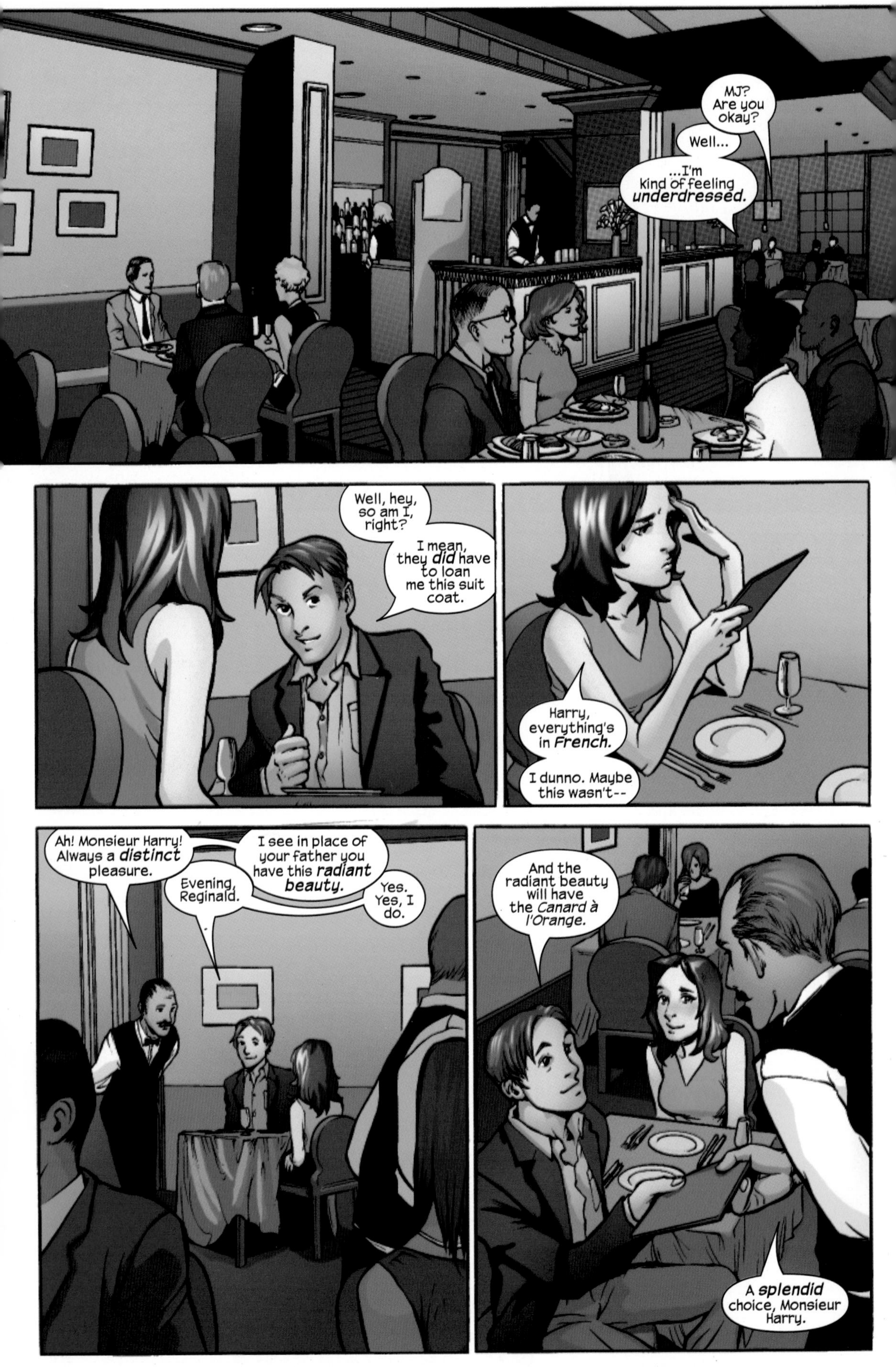
MJ? Are you okay?
Well...
...I'm kind of feeling underdressed.
Well, hey, so am I, right?
I mean, they did have to loan me this suit coat.
Harry, everything's in French.
I dunno. Maybe this wasn't--
Ah! Monsieur Harry! Always a distinct pleasure.
Evening, Reginald.
I see in place of your father you have this radiant beauty.
Yes. Yes, I do.
And the radiant beauty will have the Canard à l'Orange.
A splendid choice, Monsieur Harry.

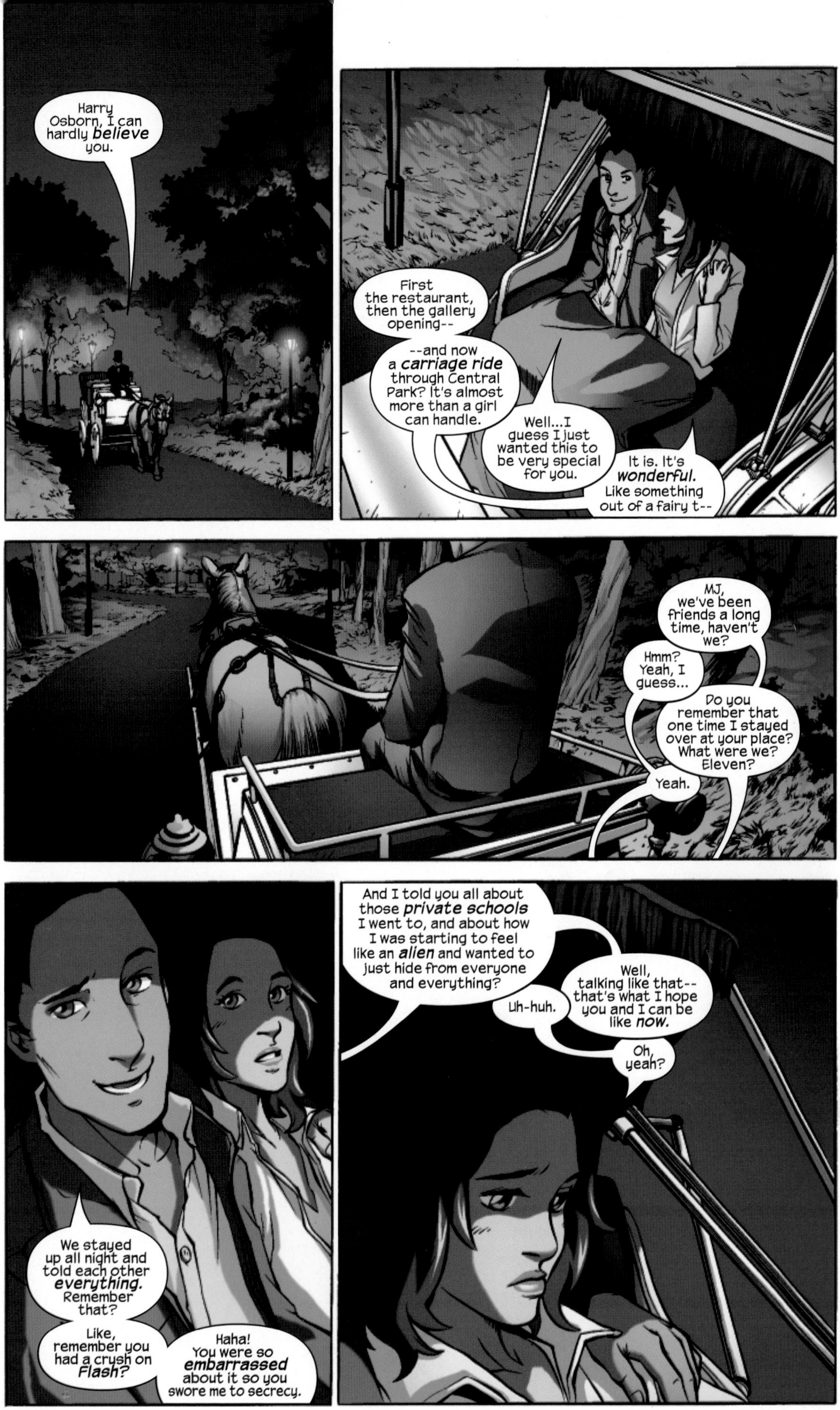

Harry Osborn, I can hardly *believe* you.
First the restaurant, then the gallery opening--
--and now a *carriage ride* through Central Park? It's almost more than a girl can handle.
Well...I guess I just wanted this to be very special for you.
It is. It's *wonderful.* Like something out of a fairy t--
MJ, we've been friends a long time, haven't we?
Hmm? Yeah, I guess...
Do you remember that one time I stayed over at your place? What were we? Eleven?
Yeah.
We stayed up all night and told each other *everything.* Remember that?
Like, remember you had a crush on *Flash?*
Haha! You were so *embarrassed* about it so you swore me to secrecy.
And I told you all about those *private schools* I went to, and about how I was starting to feel like an *alien* and wanted to just hide from everyone and everything?
Uh-huh.
Well, talking like that--that's what I hope you and I can be like *now.*
Oh, yeah?

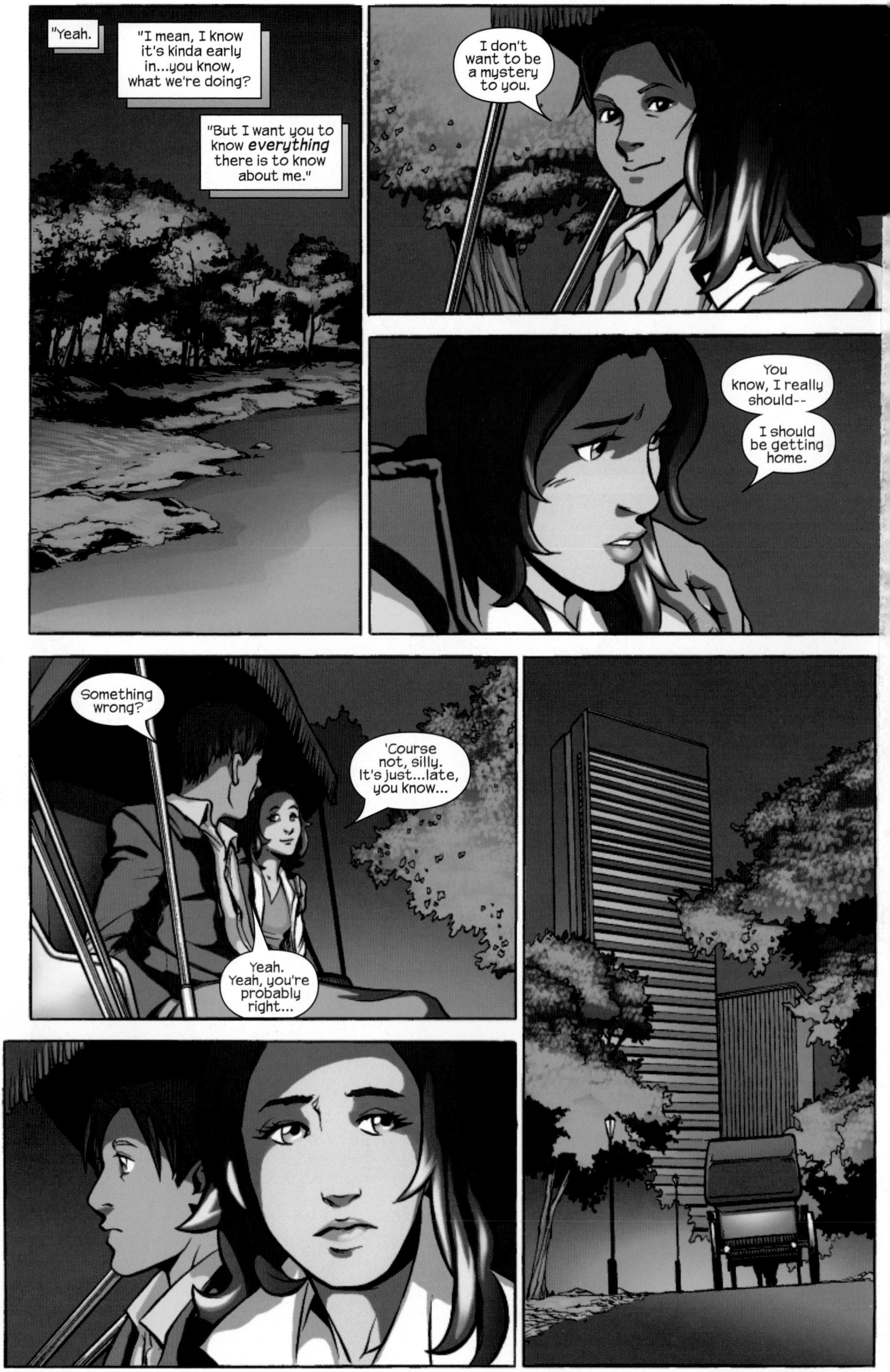
"Yeah.
"I mean, I know it's kinda early in...you know, what we're doing?
"But I want you to know *everything* there is to know about me."
I don't want to be a mystery to you.
You know, I really should--
I should be getting home.
Something wrong?
'Course not, silly. It's just...late, you know...
Yeah. Yeah, you're probably right...

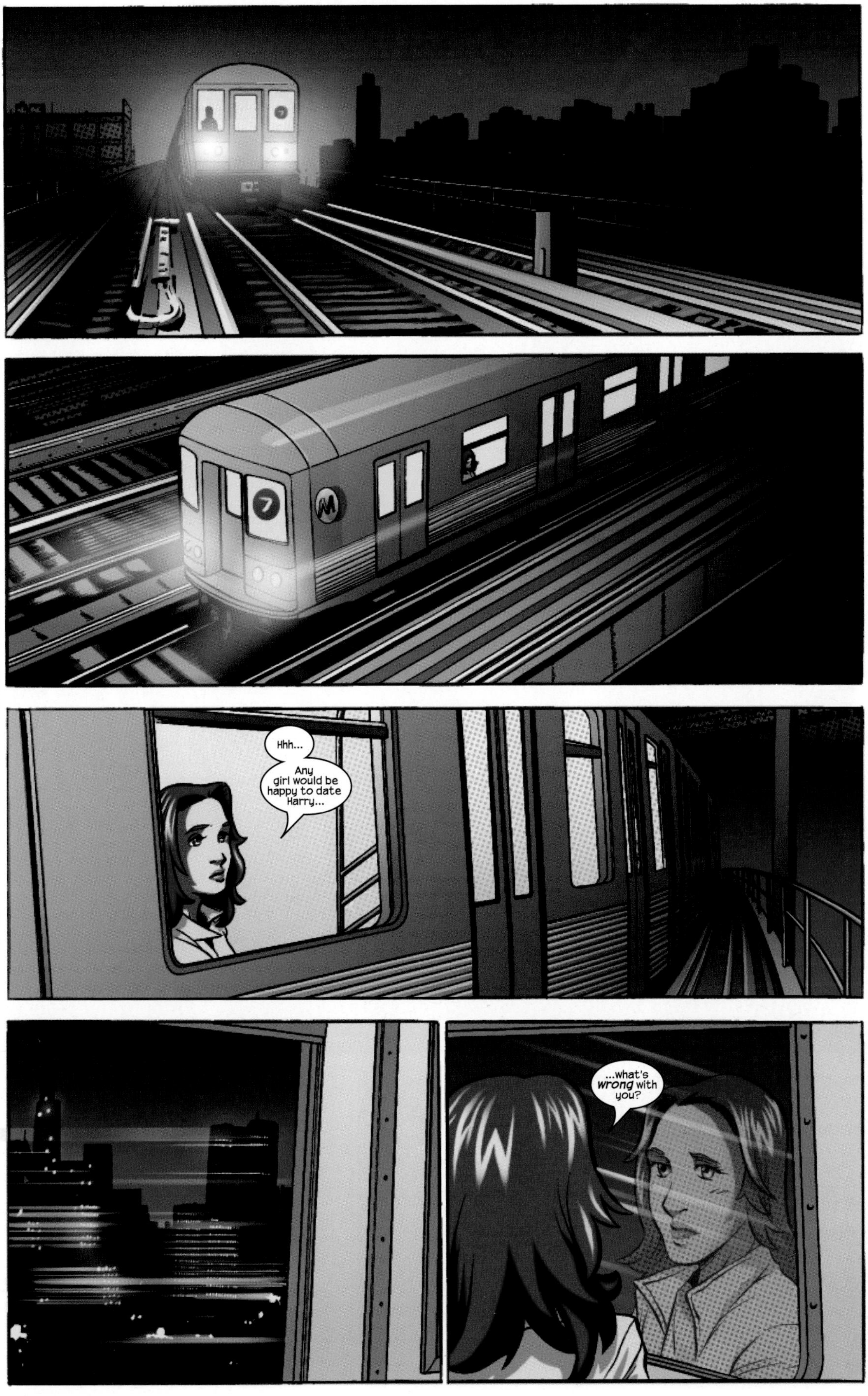
Hhh...
Any girl would be happy to date Harry...
...what's *wrong* with you?

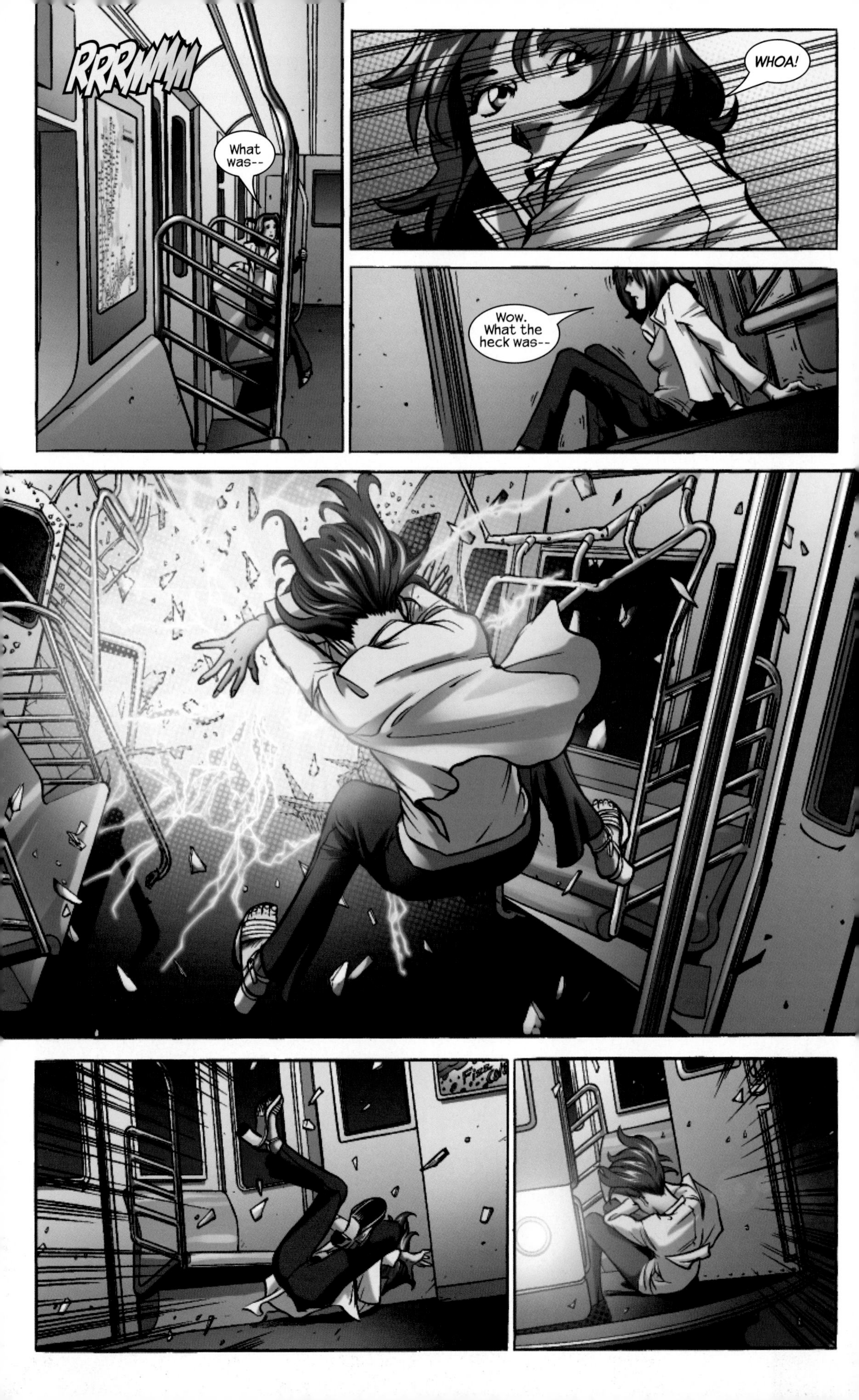
RRRMMM
What was--
WHOA!
Wow. What the heck was--

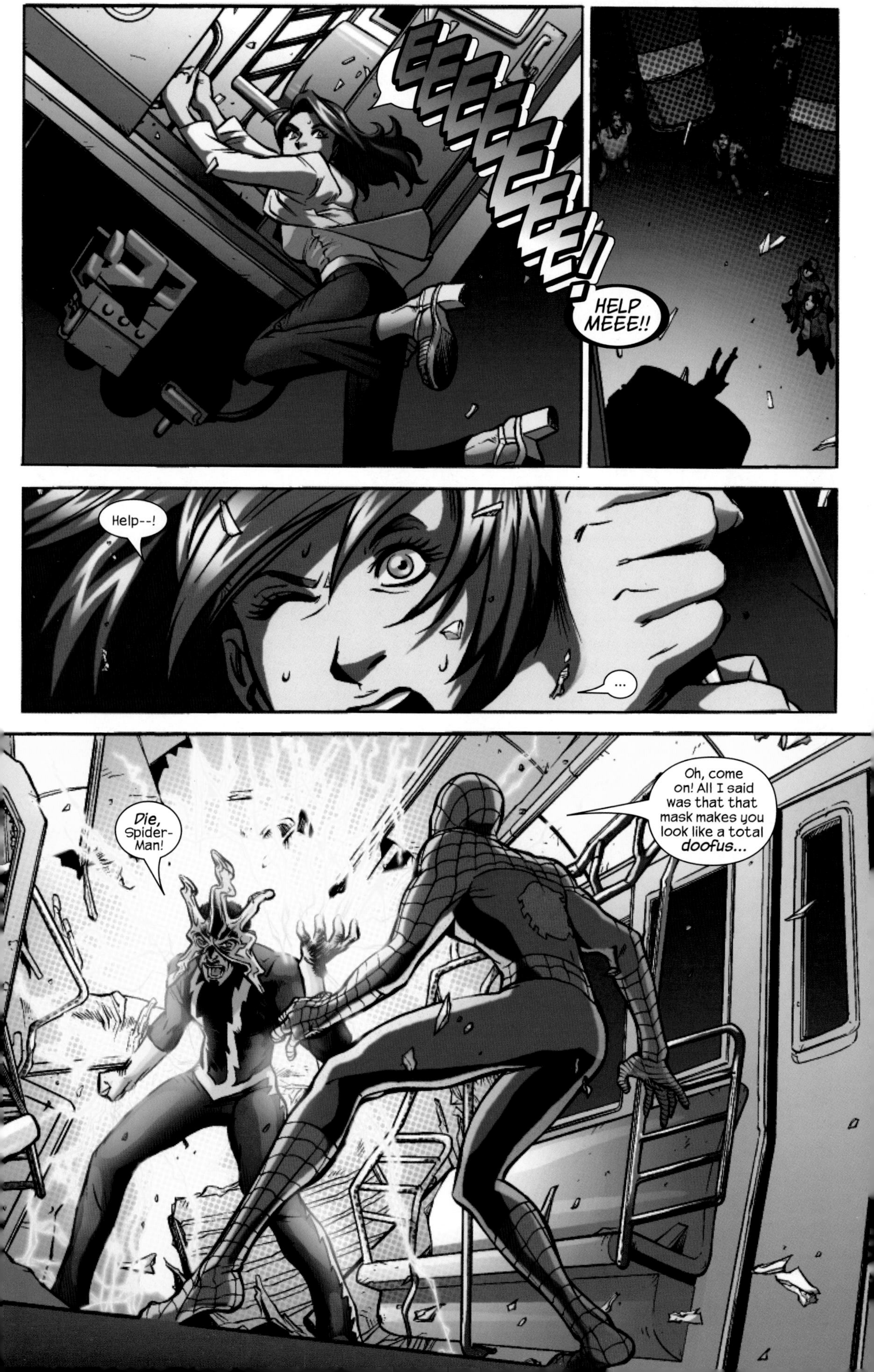
EEEEEEEE!!
HELP MEEE!!
Help--!
...
Die, Spider-Man!
Oh, come on! All I said was that that mask makes you look like a total *doofus*...

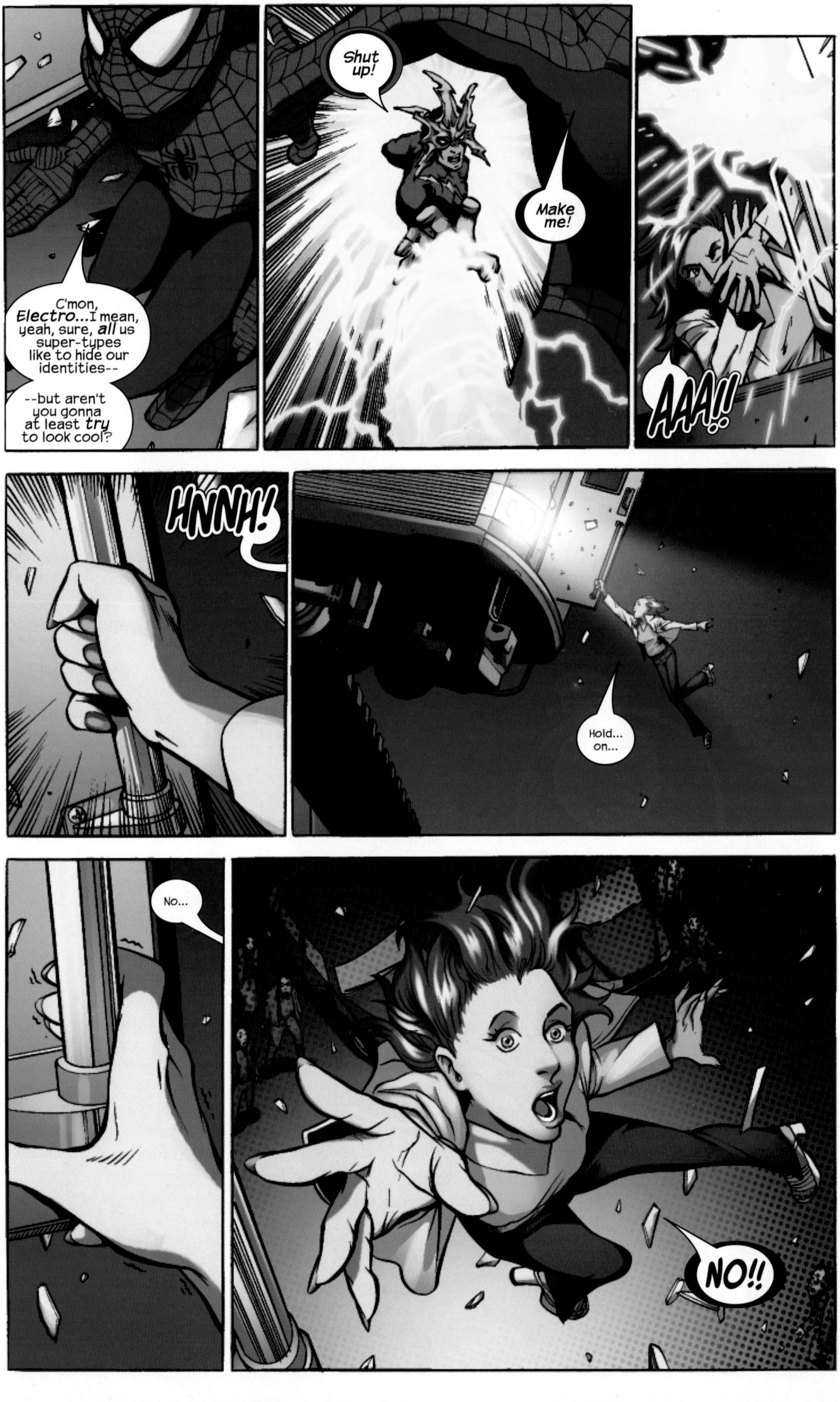

C'mon, Electro... I mean, yeah, sure, all us super-types like to hide our identities--
--but aren't you gonna at least try to look cool?
Shut up!
Make me!
AAA!!
HNNH!
Hold... on...
No...
NO!!

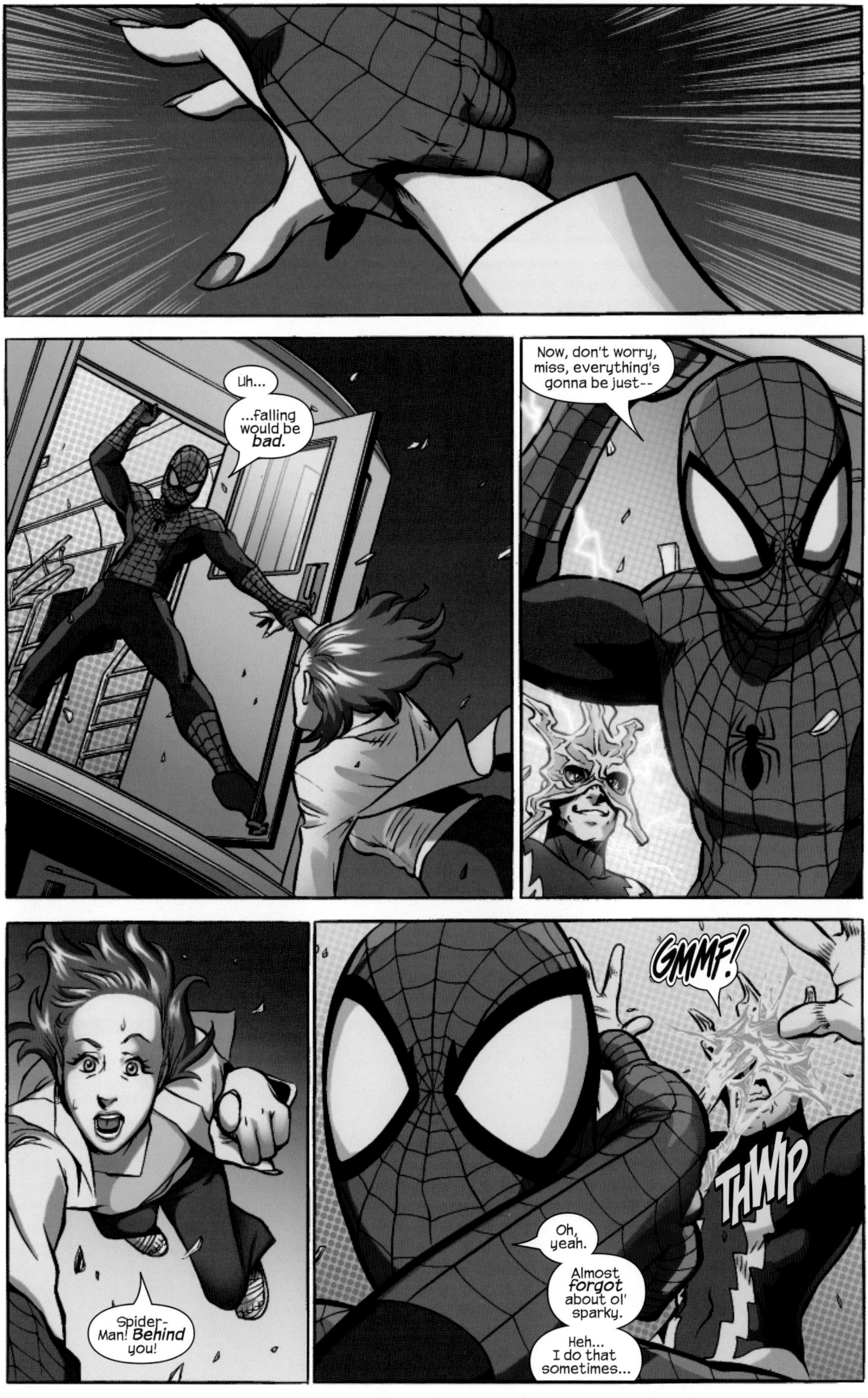
Uh...
...falling would be bad.
Now, don't worry, miss, everything's gonna be just--
Spider-Man! Behind you!
GMMF!
THWIP
Oh, yeah.
Almost forgot about ol' sparky.
Heh... I do that sometimes...

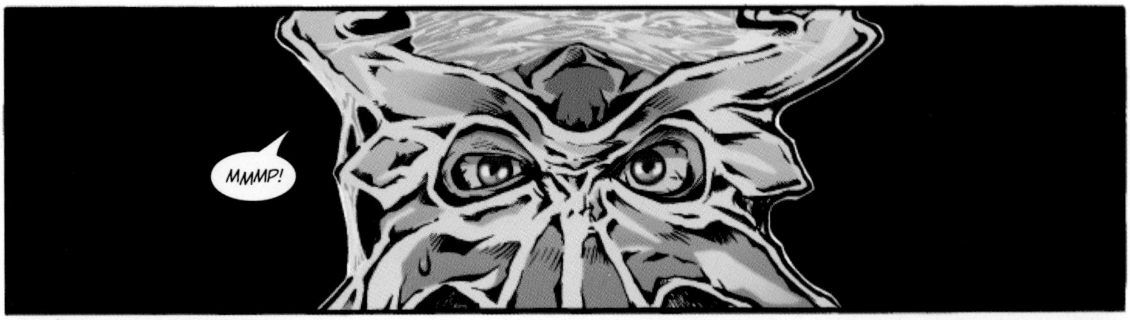
MMMP!

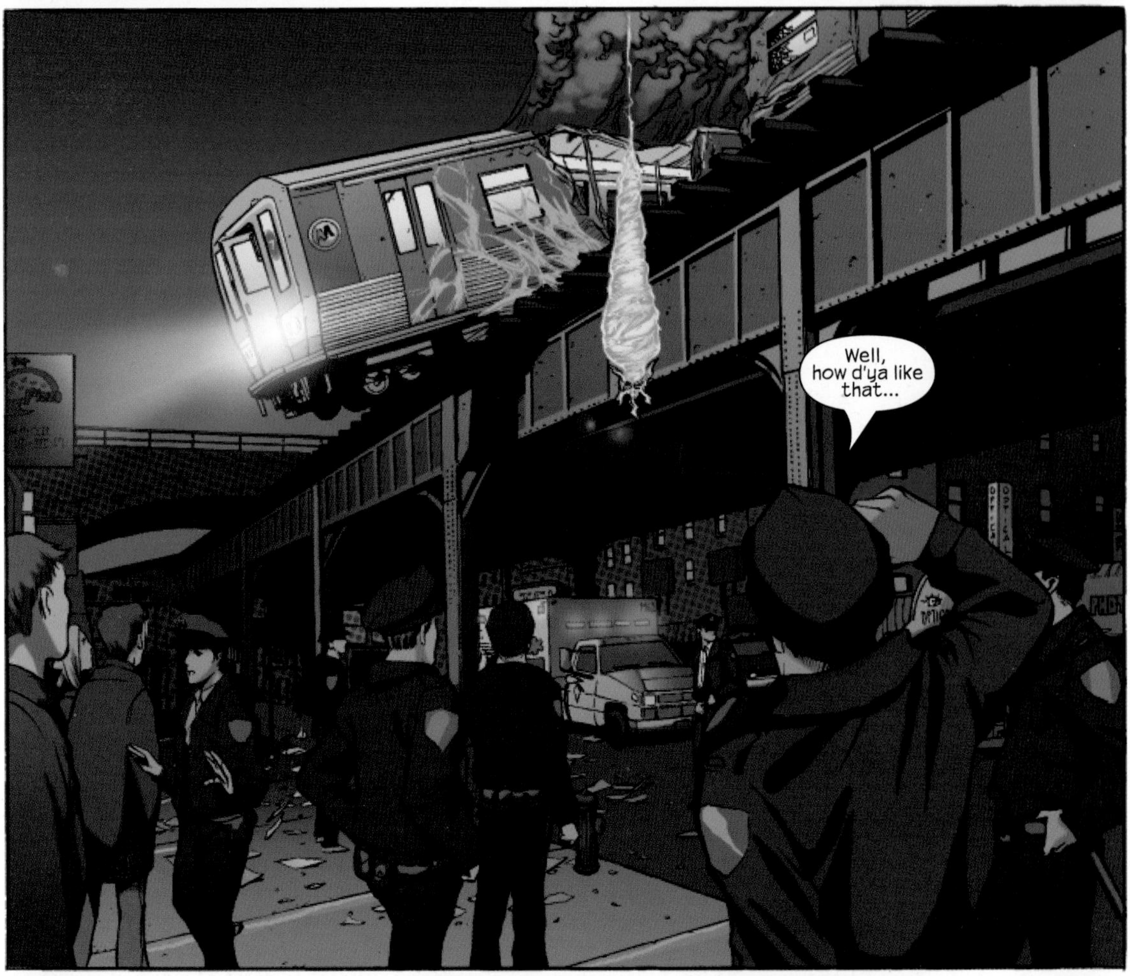
Well, how d'ya like that...

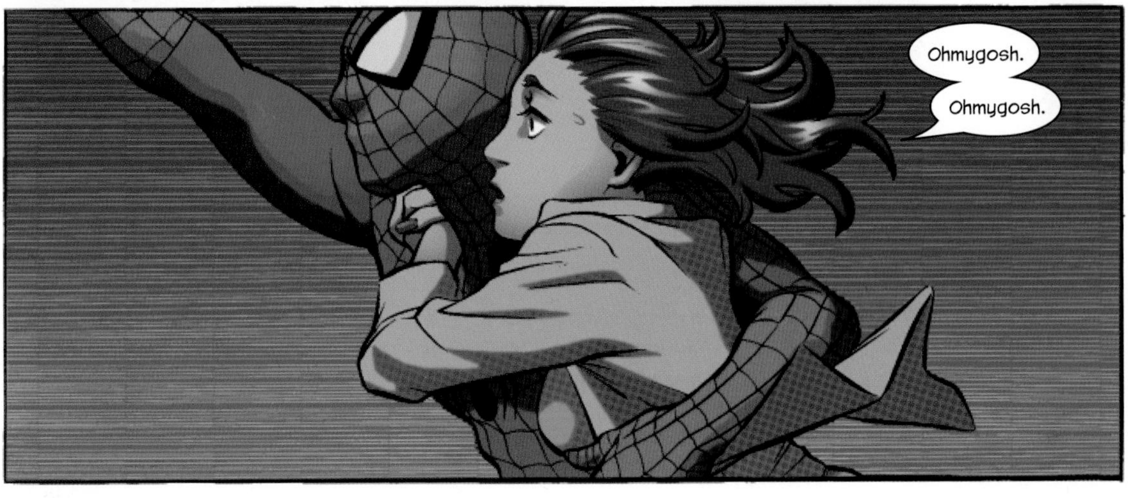
Ohmygosh.
Ohmygosh.

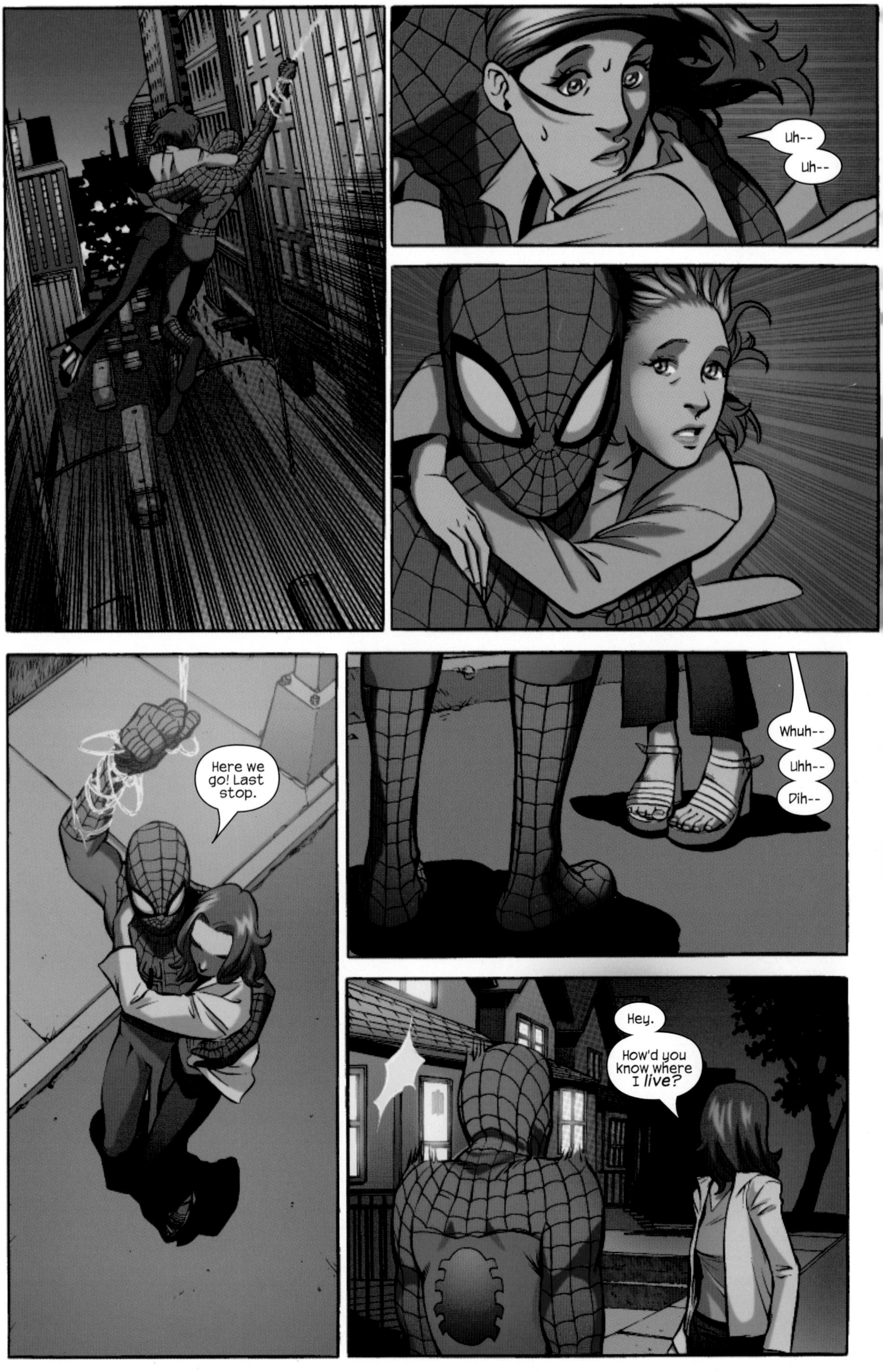
Uh--
Uh--
Here we go! Last stop.
Whuh--
Uhh--
Dih--
Hey.
How'd you know where I *live*?

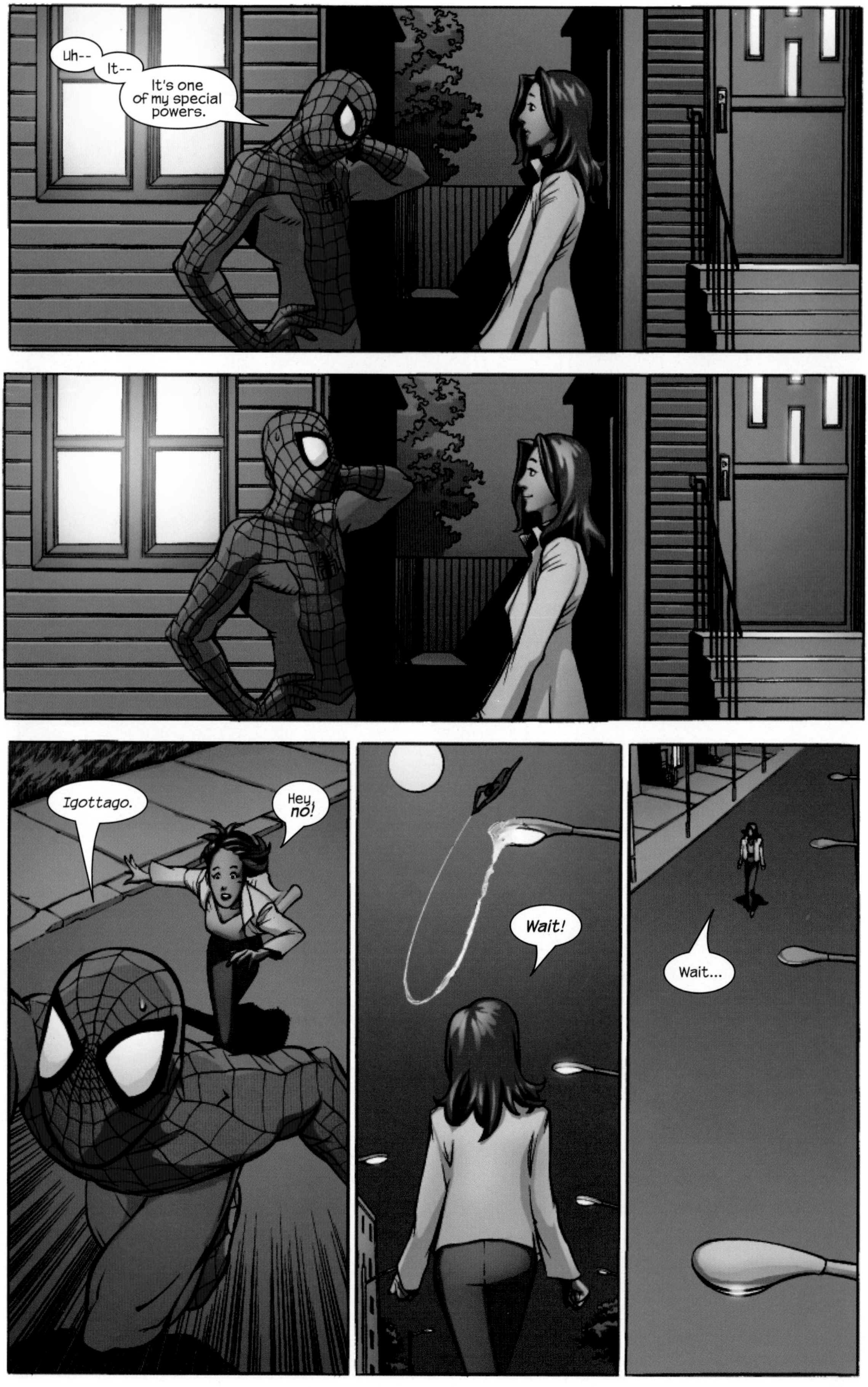
Uh--
It--
It's one of my special powers.
Igottago.
Hey, no!
Wait!
Wait...

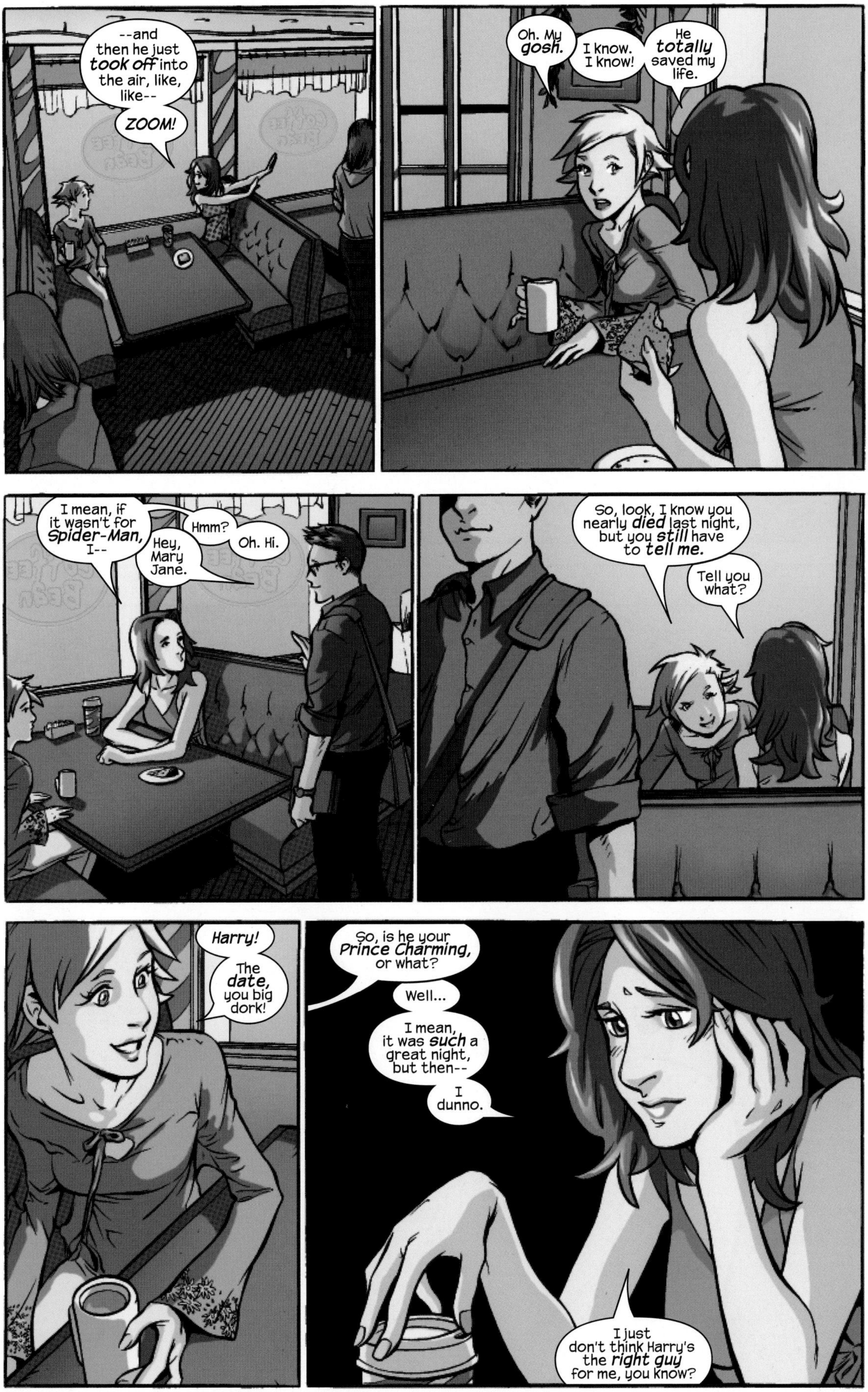

--and then he just took off into the air, like, like--
ZOOM!
Oh. My gosh.
I know. I know!
He totally saved my life.
I mean, if it wasn't for Spider-Man, I--
Hmm?
Hey, Mary Jane.
Oh. Hi.
So, look, I know you nearly died last night, but you still have to tell me.
Tell you what?
Harry!
The date, you big dork!
So, is he your Prince Charming, or what?
Well...
I mean, it was such a great night, but then--
I dunno.
I just don't think Harry's the right guy for me, you know?

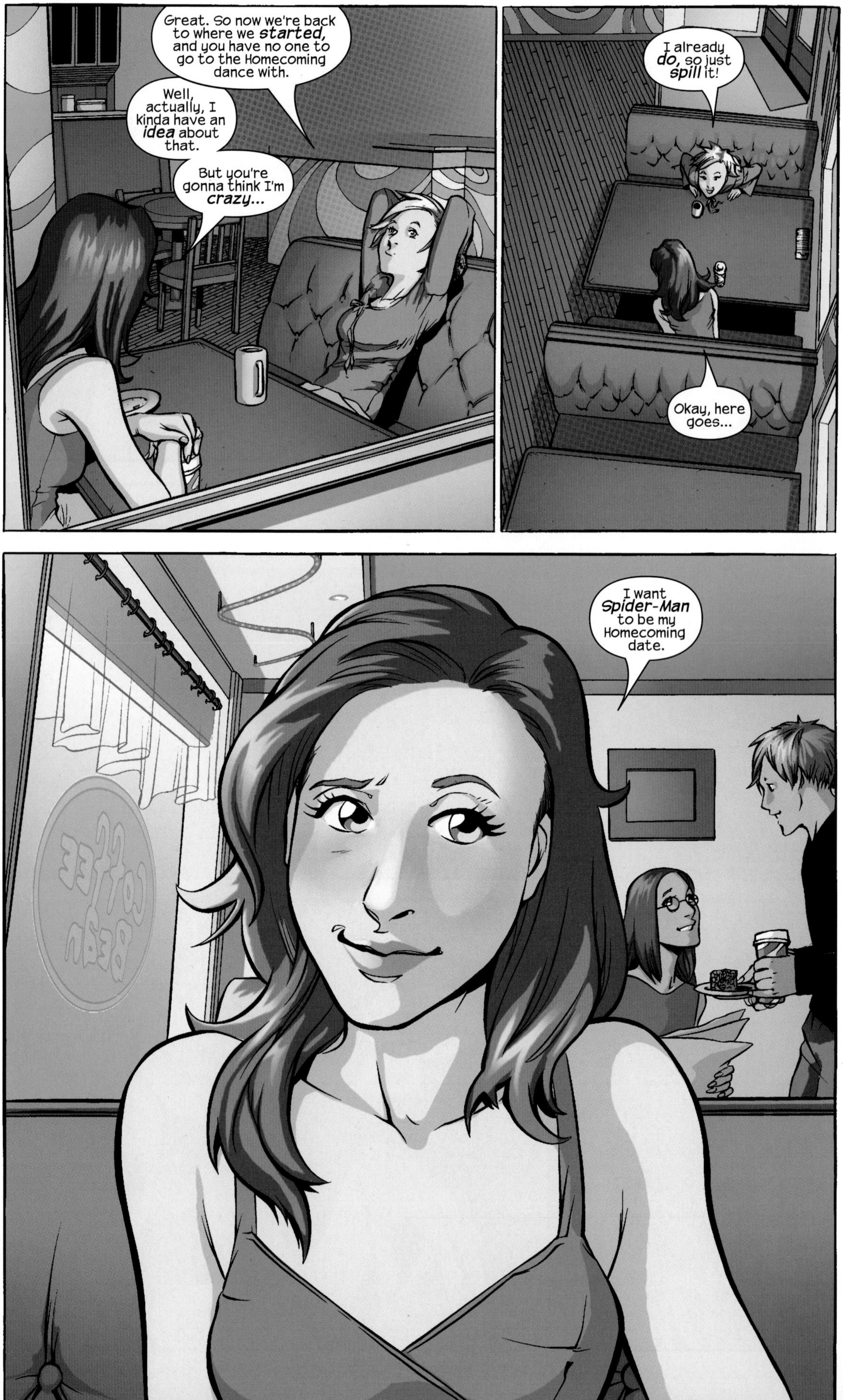
Great. So now we're back to where we *started,* and you have no one to go to the Homecoming dance with.
Well, actually, I kinda have an *idea* about that.
But you're gonna think I'm *crazy...*
I already *do,* so just *spill* it!
Okay, here goes...
I want *Spider-Man* to be my Homecoming date.